MW00943705

There's No Place Like My Own *Home*

By Florenza Lee

Cover Design by Sofania

Interior Design by FxandColor Design

There's No Place Like My Own Home
A Young Reader Chapter Book highlighting the importance of kindness, hope, hard work, acceptance, and the bonds of friendship and family for ages 9 - 13.

This book is an excellent addition to classrooms for Social Studies (Law and Government), Sociology, Language Arts (Reasoning, Speaking, Listening), Writing, and Health (Personal Health).

Words to Ponder Publishing Company, LLC
Printed in the United States of America
For more information, visit https://www.florenza.org

Text and Illustrations copyright @ 2019 by Words to Ponder Publishing Company, LLC.
Text design and cover art by Sofania.
Interior designs by FxandColors Design.
First Paperback
Address inquiries to Contact@florenza.org
Softcover Book Version ISBN 978-1-941328-10-1

eBook Version ISBN: 978-1-941328-15-6

Published Titles by Florenza include:

Adventurous Olivia's Alphabet Quest
Barry Bear's Very Best, Learning to Say No to Negative Influences
Hoku to the Rescue
The Tail of Max the Mindless Dog, A Children's Book on Mindfulness
There's No Place Like My Own Home
Welcome Home Daddy Love, Lexi

Children's Books coming soon are:

Acornsville, Land of the Secret Seed Keepers
Amiri's Birthday Wish
Micah and Malik's Super Awesome Excellent Adventure
Oh, My Goodness, Look at this Big Mess
Two Bees in a Hive
When Life Gives Us Wind

Young Reader Chapter Books coming soon are:

Two-Thirds is a Whole

For more information regarding Florenza's books, or to contact her to speak at your school or event, please visit www.florenza.org. Regarding ways you may assist the homeless in your community, visit, https://hhweek.org/ for more information.

Dedication Page

—⟪⟪❋⟫⟫—

I dedicate this book to my family,
Trefus, Jessica, and Missy
for being my first and loudest cheerleaders.

Christine Bush, thank you for planting the seed for this beautiful
story to become a reality, and for the usage of the Valoha name
and mission. May you continue to do great things for those who,
similarly to Alyssa, are currently without shelter yet anticipate
unbelievable results are destined to come their way.

Florenza

Acknowledgment

Firstly, I acknowledge my amazingly supportive family! Trefus, Jessica, Missy, and yes, even Hoku, I could not do what I do without your love and assistance. Next, I acknowledge the hard work and dedication of those who come alongside to lend their talents, gifts, encouragement, support, correction, energy, and "all other needs as required."

Lastly, I want to thank my awesomely patient editors who appropriately dress my words, so they are prepared for the eyes of my fabulous readers! I may, at times, appear to not be paying attention, but I am. I sincerely thank each one of you, from the bottom of my heart!

Florenza

Foreword

Hawai'i has the highest homeless rate per capita in the United States. There are over 6,000 persons experiencing homelessness on any given day, as reported by Continuums of Care to the U.S. Department of Housing and Urban Development (HUD) in 2018. Out of those 6,000 persons, over 4,000 are children.

As a licensed therapist and the founder of Valoha, the non-profit organization mentioned within the pages of this remarkable book, I am in awe of the way that Florenza addresses homelessness with such clarity and conciseness. She brought the characters and their plight to life in a simplistic yet realistic manner. Ms. Lee humanized this homelessness epidemic by making the reader understand that "homelessness" can happen to anyone.

Florenza is not only a prolific writer but is also a motivational speaker, certified life coach, and a mentor to many new writers. Ms. Lee's books are always educational, inspiring, entertaining, and fun to read.

This book is for anyone who thinks that one person cannot make a difference. One person CAN change a life, but many people work towards a common goal can change the world.

Christine E. Bush, LMHC

Founder of Valoha Giving Movement

"Hold fast to dreams,

For if dreams die

Life is a broken-winged bird,

That cannot fly."

~ Langston Hughes

Table Of Contents

First Day Of School. 1

Tummy Rumble 5

Laughter Is Good Medicine. 11

It's Only Temporary 17

A Banana, A Mango, And Raspberry Tea 23

Yellow Blouse 27

Letting Go. 31

Classroom Visitor 35

Last One On, First One Off 39

A Sign Over The Door. 43

Just You Wait. 47

Easy Isn't Best And Best Isn't Easy 49

To Busseyville And Beyond 53

Livable For Everyone 57

And Nothing But The Truth 63

After School Meeting. 67

Families Like Ours 69

Chin Up, Chest Out, Head High. 71

Community Affair 75

Epilogue 77

First Day Of School

"**A**lyssa, don't forget to grab your bookbag."

"Yes, Ma'am."

Today is the first day of my new class.

I'm so thrilled, but slightly apprehensive, too. I am not anxious about school; I'm passionate about learning, as in I LOVE it. Today, I am nervous because this is not only a new class, it is a new school as well. We were forced to relocate when we lost our home.

I miss my old house.

My bedroom.

My toys.

My friends.

MY LIFE!

Mom firmly believes even though we no longer live there, if we have breath in our bodies, we have everything we need. I know she is right, but boy, do I miss the way things used to be.

Patiently, we await the arrival of the school bus. As a reminder Mom says, "Remember to say, 'Yes, Ma'am' to your new teacher, raise your hand if you have the answer, eat all your lunch, and bring home your homework."

At the mention of the word home, a gloomy expression comes over her face. The bus is approaching, so we can't discuss what just happened; instead, I give her an extra tight embrace.

From my bus seat, I watch through the dirt-streaked window as she slowly makes her way to our car. She must go to work now. I place my hand on the glass as we drive past her. She doesn't see me; her head is down as she slouches behind the steering wheel. She looks as if she is crying. I silently whisper a prayer for her to have the strength she needs for today.

Wiping away the tear that is trying to escape my eye, I divert my attention to something else. I glance at the other kids on the bus with me. Many are wearing new outfits and footwear; they also have brightly colored bookbags, some with tags still hanging from them.

I glimpse down at my shoes. They are not new. My dress is clean, but it is wrinkled and not new. My bookbag is the same one I have used since third grade. Subconsciously, I slide it under my seat with my not-so-new sneakers.

"Hey, girl, hey," sings a voice from behind me. I turn to see a girl with gigantic afro puff ponytails and a humongous grin. Her hair is stunning! I never have in all my life seen hair that huge.

I awkwardly wave, then blurt out, "Wow, your hair is phenomenal." My comment resembles a squeak more than a statement. Embarrassed, I quickly turn to stare out the window again.

"Thank you!" she responds while patting her hair and quickly plopping down in the empty seat beside me. "Are you new? I don't remember seeing you before."

She smells adorable, similar to the tropical flower section of the botanical garden, my dad and I used to visit. Great hair and she smells

2

nice, too! Feeling uncomfortable with my lack of personal space, I shift a bit in my seat, easing closer to the window.

"Are you new?" she repeats, only a bit louder this time. Gazing downward, I nod yes. "I'm Onika," she introduces herself, extending her hand to shake mine. Onika's friendliness puts me at ease. I stop attempting to become one with the side of the bus and shift towards her.

While chatting, I discover we are the same age and grade. Even better, we are both in Ms. Thompson's class. Onika promises that I will adore Ms. T., as they call her, by stating she is a marvelous teacher. Knowing I will be in the same classroom with this friendly girl and have an exceptional teacher causes me to smile. Today is already turning out to be a spectacular first day.

Tummy Rumble

After giving me the grand tour, Onika and I put away our belongings in our lockers. "Let's have breakfast," she suggests. "Everyone goes to the cafeteria to eat; it's our hangout spot." As she is speaking, my stomach makes a horrible growling sound, and she hears it! I am embarrassed, but before I  could look away, she chuckles and explains, "Your tummy is identical to my tummy! Let's go give them some food."

While in line, waiting for a girl wearing a tie-dyed sweater and rainbow leggings to decide if she wants a kiwi or a peach, a boy with messy blonde hair and a denim jacket shoves past us, snatches his food, then loudly flops down.

"What the heck, idiot!" Onika yells at him, "you stepped on my new kicks! Didn't your mother ever teach you manners? Don't worry about him," she informs me, "his name is Marcus, a wannabe bully. He is in our class, too, but in there he knows not to misbehave. Ms. T. doesn't take any foolishness." She directs the last part straight at Marcus. Sensing someone is staring at him, he yanks his head back to flip his hair from his eyes, turns our way, and sticks out his tongue.

Ignoring him, we sit down to eat as Onika gives me the inside scoop about the school, the other students in our class, and info on the cute boys. Giggling, I lower my head and blush, and she does too. The warning bell rings, and we put our rubbish and trays away and then head to class, Onika showing me a shortcut. I observe all the artwork and assignments of other students proudly displayed on the hallway walls. Memories of my work featured at my last school flood my mind.

My previous teacher, Mrs. Lowry, assigned the class a Social Studies project. We compiled a list of words that mean the same as home, then designed artwork, including images and information about our family, pets, etc. It was my best creation ever! Thinking of how the meaning of the word home has changed for me over the past few months saddens me greatly.

I must have slowed my stride because Onika glances back at me and inquires, "Hey, are you alright?" Picking up my pace, I nod as we walk into my new classroom. The one place that will hopefully be consistent in my topsy-turvy world. Just think, some kids act like they will die the first day of school. Well, not literally, only figuratively. During summer break, they have so much fun hanging out with their friends, playing video games, going on family vacations to exotic places, visiting grandparents, etc., they get all frazzled when the time comes to buy school supplies. The thought of going back to school makes them downright miserable. For me, it is just the opposite. School is my haven, it is consistent; it is my home away from home.

"Welcome, everyone," announces Ms. T. as we waltz through the door, "I am happy you will be spending this school year with me. Please raise your hand if you are new to Lee Ponder Middle School."

I reluctantly raise my hand as three others raise theirs: one girl and two boys.

"Marvelous," she beams, "I will assign each of you a Newcomers Sponsor. They will assist as you learn your way around our school and will answer any questions you may have. Consider them your tour guide to all things Lee Ponder!"

Before she might say anything else, Onika quickly raises her hand then blurts out, "Excuse me, Ms. T., may I select a student to sponsor?"

"Of course, Onika, you may go first."

Disappointed, I huff — much louder than I intended — as I slump in my seat and lower my head; I pretend to be interested in the nicks and scratches on the desk. I just know Onika wants to sponsor the other new girl; she has afro puffs, too, and she is wearing a floral dress with sleeves that resemble wings. Her earrings, necklace, and matching bracelets have colorful crystal butterflies. Every time she moves her head, the butterflies' wings glitter and sparkle; they make faint tinkling sounds, similar to Tinkerbell in the movie Peter Pan. I just know they shop at the same boutique.

While still faking interest in the previous mistreatment of my desk, and wondering why I am suddenly such a brat, I detect a slight tap on my shoulder; I hear, "Hey girl, I never even got your name, earlier. If it's cool with you, I want to be your guide!"

Instantly smiling, I practically sing out my response, "My name is Alyssa. I would love for you to be my sponsor."

"All right then," states Ms. T. "Kimble is Cierra's sponsor; Brady is Darryl's. And, let's see, David, your sponsor is Daymeon. Now that everyone has their sponsors, let's prepare ourselves for a spectacular week."

As we settle in, Ms. T. announces, "Each year, as a class, we select the theme for our blackboard wall." She then points to an area at the back of the room. "Together, we will create exciting ways to incorporate the messages on the board with our lesson plans. Please take a few minutes to think about ideas and suggestions you wish to view on the wall, then jot them down on the paper that Mary will pass around."

As if on cue, Mary stands up and passes out strips of paper to each of us. I contemplate for a few seconds and consider writing down homelessness as a subject but quickly dismiss that thought altogether! Instead, I pen a word, my dad said all the time. Neatly folding my paper in half, I await Mary to retrace her steps and collect my response.

"Has everyone submitted their suggestions?" asks Ms. T. When everyone nods yes, she says, "Excellent." Gently shaking the bag, Ms. T. walks to Cierra's desk and asks that she does the honor of selecting for the class. Proudly, Cierra chooses a single piece of paper, unfolds it then smiles as she reads, "The subject for the blackboard wall is, kindness."

"That was my answer," I mentally cheer, "we will be creating a wall that would make Dad proud!"

"Fantabulous! It has been a while since we have had kindness as our subject."

Raising my hand, first, I ask, "Ms. T., what exactly are we allowed to place on the wall?"

"Alyssa, we will have random acts of kindness and imaginative ways to encourage and support one another. Our first activity is to create motivational rocks. Class, please proceed one aisle at a time to the back counter and select three stones. Draw a smiley face on one side and a word of encouragement on the other side. Two rocks will go in the basket near the blackboard wall, the other you will place throughout the school or community for others to discover. Be creative with your words; you only have a limited space with which to write, it is a rock, not a boulder! Be intentional."

Taking my time to illustrate the eyes and smiles just so — I even design one with a goofy crooked grin — I then turn them over and write family with a tiny heart on one, believe on the other, and finally hope on the third. I randomly place two in the basket and keep the last one to put in the café. I am enjoying this activity and cannot wait to see what other projects we do for kindness.

The day zooms by. Before I realize it, it's time to board the bus to return home.

"Hey, Alyssa," inquires Onika as we're taking our seats on the bus, "how would you rate your first day?"

"I would give it three thumbs up! I had a fabulous day. Thank you for asking."

"I am so glad. I told you, you'd adore Ms. T. She is known for her creativity and devising ways to reinforce learning with fun activities. Her previous students say it is similar to being in art class 24/7! I am not very imaginative, but the opportunity to be artsy-fartsy sounds delightful!"

"I'm not that creative either; learning with art sounds like a lot of fun," I reply.

Do you wanna come over to my house to do homework? I live very close to where you board the bus," invites Onika.

"Ummmm, thank you for asking, but... I have to assist my mom with chores," I tell her then quickly turn my head to glance out the window. I don't want her to know that I'm not speaking truthfully.

Oblivious to my deception, she suggests, "OK, maybe another time."

As we ride the bus home, she describes the neighborhood, community pool, block parties, and how the neighbors get together for the holidays, especially Halloween and the Fourth of July. Onika reveals she has lived here her entire life. It sounds delightful.

She is saying, "Everyone gets together around a bonfire to pass out candy on Halloween; It is a blast. Each year, the neighborhood holds a contest to select the best-decorated yard and the child with the most creative costume. One year, my dad turned our entire yard into a haunted house. It took nearly two weeks to set everything up; it was better than any haunted house I've ever gone to! My cousins and some people from my dad's job dressed up to scare people as they walked through the mazes. I'm not gonna lie! Initially, I was terrified to walk through it! Curiosity got the better of me, and I had to experience it for myself. I am thrilled that I did. It was stellar! Who knows, maybe we will do it again this year, and you can assist me in scaring the little kids in the neighborhood!"

"That sounds unbelievable!" I exclaim. Onika continues to tell me all about the neighborhood and why it is such a beautiful place to live.

When I exit the bus, my mom is waiting for me. I wave as soon as I see her, and she waves back. Onika also waves to her from her seat on the bus.

Laughter Is Good Medicine

"How was your first day?" Mom inquires as soon as I'm standing next to her. She smells like fried food and cleaning products.

"It was stupendous!" I exclaim, "I met a girl with great hair named Onika, and my teacher, Ms. T. — you would adore her — is super nice! She is tall, about your age, and has a trendy, short hairstyle the color of salt and pepper. She also wears geometrically shaped glasses — the kids say glasses are her thing. She incorporates crafts into all of her lessons, I believe I am going to enjoy this school a whole lot, maybe even better than my other one!" I am babbling, and am so animated, I look like I'm auditioning for a caffeinated drink commercial.

Patiently listening and awaiting my enthusiasm to subside a bit, Mom's voice shifts as if searching for words. After a few moments of awkward silence, she glances my way and gently says, "Sweetie, I am thrilled you enjoy attending the school, but remember, we may have to relocate again if we can't find housing to remain in this school district."

I was so thrilled my first day, I completely disregarded our living situation. As the air seeps from my happy bubble, I drop my head and mumble my understanding. I then ease into the passenger seat and silently fasten my seatbelt. Lately, home for us is the parking lot of the local truck stop or Wal-Shop. There are usually huge trucks and other cars parked with people who are traveling long distances who don't want to stay in hotels. Mom believes they are the safest locations for us right now.

We sit inside the café of a nearby truck stop as Mom recounts her day at work — she is a waitress at the local restaurant. It was a productive day. She received decent tips and brought home a good meal. We say grace before starting, and as we eat,  I complete my homework assignment. Before the café closes for the night, we take clothes out of the trunk of our vehicle, then go into the restroom to wash our faces and brush our teeth. We walk back to the car, lock the doors, recline both front seats, and go to sleep. It isn't ideal, but the alternative is far worse. There are families, in situations similar to ours who don't even have the safety of an automobile, they sleep in bus stations, doorways, near trash bins or worse.

That night, I dream I am back in my old house, and my dad is there too. He was the best dad ever. He was considerate, and everyone adored him. He was the person who made the crowds laugh. No matter what kind of day you were experiencing, my dad would find a way to make you smile. His favorite method was by telling one of his famous not so funny knock-knock jokes. In my dream, he is in the middle of one,

"Knock! Knock!" Dad is already laughing at his joke.

"Who's there?" I respond.

"Candice."

"Candice who?"

"Candice door open, or am I stuck out here?"

After catching his breath, he chimes, "Ali, laughter is like medicine; it does your soul good!" Then he grabs me, raises me over his head, and twirls me around. We both roar with laughter, not little giggles; we let out full-on belly laughs. It was my absolute favorite thing to do with my dad.

Waking, I glance around and realize, it was only a dream. I am not safe in my daddy's arms, listening to him telling me a corny joke; instead, I am in the front seat of our car. Still thinking about my father and our old house. I whisper, "I miss you, Daddy, more than words could ever say." Before I realize it, it's time to get to the bus stop. Once onboard, I settle into a seat next to Onika.

"Hey girl, hey," she cheers as I plop down beside her.

I adore how she announces that.

"Geez, you almost missed the bus."

"I overslept," I fib, not giving any additional explanation.

We chat about our homework, then she rattles nonstop about a reality TV show that she is addicted to watching. I nod in agreeance as if I know all about it, but really, I don't. Even if I had a TV set, it's highly unlikely I'd watch a show such as the one she is going on about, but that is not relevant. I simply enjoy the sound of her voice; she has a funny way of saying certain words. My dad would have adored Onika. Similar to him, she finds gratification in making people smile. In the car, it is just Mom and me, and although we have great discussions, it is different conversating with someone my age. I tell Onika my dad's knock-knock joke, and she laughs out loud. She has a great laugh. Yep, my dad would have adored her.

After breakfast in our hang-out spot — I enjoy saying that — we walk to our classroom; already, the day is off to a wondrous start.

Once we settle at our desks, Mrs. T. announces, "Class, you have a writing assignment with a due date of the end of next week. It's a short story about a challenge or obstacle you have faced, and the steps you took to overcome it. The assignment is also a Public Speaking project, so be creative! I want to see your writing skills shine bright, like diamonds."

When she utters the word diamond, the kids commence to singing like a church choir, "Shine bright like a diamond!" Onika, snapping her fingers and bobbing her head from side to side, leans over and whispers, "This is Ms. T.'s thing! Whenever she announces, 'shine bright like a diamond,' we sing it back."

"Oh, I get it now," I join in toward the end of the song.

"You all sound so beautiful," Ms. T. shouts while clapping her hands our way, "just like a choir!"

Marcus dramatically stands up and bows as he impersonates Elvis, "Why, thank you! Thank you very much!"

"Thank you, Marcus," warns Ms. T., "you may take your seat now."

"Elvis is leaving the building," he declares before finally settling down in his chair.

Onika looks at him, shakes her head, and rolls her eyes, "He is such a goofball!"

Immediately, the class is whispering, some telling what they are going to write about, others complaining about how much they dislike writing but can't wait to hear the stories others have written. With so many obstacles and hurdles in my life, my issue isn't what I am going to write about; it is in narrowing my list down to just one!

"Alyssa, did you hear about the tornado in Alabama?" inquires Onika as we sit eating lunch.

"No, I didn't hear about it, but that is so sad!" I say between bites of cheese and pepperoni pizza. "How bad of a storm was it?"

"It was awful! All those unfortunate people are now homeless." She whispers the last word as if it's forbidden to speak out loud. "It is such a shame. I saw it on the news. My mom thinks we should do something like put together care-packages and send them over. She is talking to our church congregation to see if we can take up a collection for them."

"Collection?" I ask. "What's that?"

After taking a few sips of her peach flavored sweet tea, she explains, "A collection is when we 'collect' money. We sometimes call them offerings. A collection could also be food, clothes, or items they may need, such as water, toiletries, etc."

As she talks, I want to disclose that I am homeless, too, but I don't know her that well yet. What if she hates me after I tell her and discontinues our friendship? Or worse, what if she regrets choosing me and decides to sponsor Cierra instead of a homeless person like me? Since I don't know the answers to these questions, I listen silently and continue to eat my lunch. Life is no fun having to keep secrets, it is worse not knowing how someone will respond after learning what I have hid. I hope to one day know Onika well enough to share everything with her, but for now, this is my burden to carry and no one else's.

The rest of the day goes well. I enjoy this school. I feel normal here.

It's Only Temporary

The entire bus ride, kids are discussing what they are going to do when they get home. Some are going to play outside or on video games and others will be watching TV. I listen as I ride and remember my old life. I used to adore sitting in my room reading books in my big comfy chair that belonged to my grandmother. The chair made an awful, squeaking sound, but I didn't mind. It was old, and I treasured it.

Mom had created a little library nook in there for me. While reading a magazine, I saw a picture of a library, and she painted my walls the same color; we looked for months until we found similar pillows and rugs to place on the floors. It was a grand room. I had every genre of books imaginable. I had vintage picture books from when I was very young, and even some that my grandma read to my mom. Mom said those were classics, and she couldn't wait for me to read them to my children. Of all that we lost when we left our home, I miss my books the most.

"STOP IT! GET OFF ME, NOW!" I hear someone yelling from the back of the bus. Glancing over my shoulder, I see Marcus leaning hard against a kid with a purple and blue mohawk haircut.

Before I can intercede on the kid's behalf, the bus driver yells out, "Hey, none of that, Marcus! I will have you removed from this bus, and you know your parents will not be pleased to hear that, again!"

'Yes, ma'am," he fakes politeness as he makes a face at the kid then high-fives his friends sitting beside him. Marcus catches me eyeing him and harshly whispers, "What're you looking at?"

"Geez, this kid is something else. He needs to get a life," I think to myself.

Mom is waiting for me when I get off the bus; she looks ecstatic. As I wave good-bye to Onika, I skip towards her. "Hey, Mom, you're smiling! What's new?"

"Oh, nothing much," she fibs with a slight grin.

"Oh, come on, Mom, quit stalling, please tell me what has you so happy?"

"Well, since you forced me to divulge, I have some positive news!" she admits, clapping her hands together. "We have been accepted into a shelter for women with children!"

Suddenly, my stomach is all twisted up. This news is terrific, but I must inquire, "Mom, will I have to change schools... again?"

Lifting my face to meet her gaze, she assures, "No, sweetie, it's not too far from here so you can still attend the same school, at least for now. And you will ride the same bus; you'll get on and off at a different stop."

Feeling reassured, I yell, "The last one to the car is a rotten egg!" Dashing to the vehicle, she describes the shelter and how she came to learn about it. Hearing her optimism again makes my heart smile. I adore the sound of her voice when she is happy. It has a little du-da beat to it — her words sort of dance along as she speaks. I envision what they would resemble while on the TV screen and a small blue ball leaping over each word as she speaks. Her head moves from side to side, her long brown hair swings back and forth, and her green eyes

18

sparkle like emeralds. Finally, I have my old mom again.

The drive to the shelter is quick, just a few minutes from the truck stop. It is not bad at all; nothing at all as I envisioned it to be. It is an apartment building, and each unit is separate from the others. There is a quaint park next door with a place to sit in the grass and read. There are trees and beautiful flowers in a flower bed. It is clean and very well maintained.

Using the key, she removes from her purse, my mom opens the front door, and we enter the building. I hear kids laughing, a barking puppy, and the sounds of different TV sets.

"We have our own space," she confesses. "It's only temporary, but we will have a bed and a kitchen. We can cook our food…"

"And take a hot shower?"

"Yes, and take a hot shower," Mom acknowledges with a smile.

Moving our items from the trunk of the car into the room feels dreamy! We inspect the tiny space then jump up and down mimicking kids at an amusement park. To some, this is nothing much, but to us, it is everything!

Once settled in, I discuss with Mom the writing assignment that's due next week. I am somewhat of an overachiever when it comes to writing assignments and usually complete them well ahead of their due dates. "No time like today," my dad would say.

"What are you going to write about?" she inquires while walking around the tiny room, inspecting everything.

"I have no idea," I reply, "there is so much I could share. The assignment is to write about a challenge we've experienced and outline the steps taken to overcome it. I don't know if I want to write about something superficial or deeply personal."

"It will all come to you, as it always does," she assures me as she puts away our last items into the small but well-used drawers.

It is nice to be inside, even if it is an apartment, and not ours. I am grateful to be able to take a hot shower. I wash my hair three times. The smell of the shampoo and conditioner is like a dream come true.

Following our dinner of mac and cheese that I assisted in making, Mom and I sit down to read. Even though we now have a TV, reading books is a family tradition we both enjoy sharing. For as long as I can remember, Mom and I have read together. It was something she and Dad started doing when they first met and continued after I was born.

"Mom," I say as I mark my place in my book before closing it, "tell me again the story of how you and Dad met."

"Oh, honey, that is my favorite story to share," she reveals as she, too, marks her place. "As you know, Dad and I went to the same high school. He was on the football team, and I was a cheerleader. Walking by him the first time, your dad caught my eye. I think he knew I was checking him out and tried hard to pretend as if he was disinterested. But I saw him glancing at me every time he passed by. Dad was so very handsome, even back then. All the other girls thought he was cute too, so of course, there was plenty of competition. I won out, though! He recognized he was getting a good deal. I know we were meant to meet so that we would have you!" she professes as she taps me on the nose. "You know, you look identical to Dad, Ali. You have his little nose, sweet smile, and thick beautiful hair. You have his soulful brown eyes, too! As a baby, he called you his mini-me! I used to be slightly envious that people said you resembled him more than me! Now, I admit, everyone was spot on. You are his twin! "

"Mommy, you think I resemble Dad?" I beam.

"I do," she confirms as she tearfully smiles.

I get all mushy hearing stories of how they met and all their delightful adventures together. They used to travel and do all sorts of remarkable things. Mostly, though, they enjoyed walking on the beach, talking, and reading. Mom ensured that no matter where they went, they always remembered to pack books.

It feels marvelous to be in a real bed again and not sleeping in the front seat of our car. I'm grateful we are safely behind locked doors, and that my mom can sleep soundly without having to worry if someone is trying to get into the vehicle. Parking between two Mack Trucks kept us out of sight, but as Mom assures, "You can never be too careful."

It hasn't been that long since I was in my very own bed, but it just seems as if it was decades ago! I don't want to entertain that thought right now. At this very moment, all I want to do is cuddle up with this blanket and sleep.

A Banana, A Mango,
And Raspberry Tea

When morning comes, I wake up confused as to where I am. Then I remember we are in a shelter. Mom is already up and dressed. While I was asleep, she must have gone out to grab a few things.

"It's not much," she explains as I enter the kitchen, "I simply wanted to pack you at least a snack to have in school today."

She has all my favorites: a banana, a mango, and a bottle of raspberry-flavored sweet tea. I run and give her a big hug.

"Thank you, Mom, but did you get yourself something, too?" I ask, glancing around.

"Yes, honey, I did. I got myself a jumbo-sized bag of sour gummy worms!" She smiles, and we chuckle. My mom is obsessed with sour gummy worms. Next to books and me, they are her favorite.

She asks if I desire to go to the other bus stop or wait for the bus to pick me up outside the building. I decide upon the other one; saying, I will get off here at the apartment after school.

Gathering our things and ensuring the doors are locked, we drive to the bus stop. On the way, we discuss her schedule for the day. She reveals she may be a bit late, then gives me a key to the apartment. I place it around my neck as we drive. It has been a while since I had a key around my neck.

"Alyssa, you are old enough to have your key to the house," I recall Dad saying. "Be sure to take great care of it," I remember it as if it was yesterday, the day I got my very own copy of our house key. It made me feel grown-up. Dad told me all the house rules and went over them again and again. As he did, he walked beside me beaming how proud he was of me. I wore my key around my neck as if it was The Heart of the Ocean, you know, that blue diamond from the movie The Titanic? I don't realize it, but I am holding the key in my hand like that now. Mom looks over at me and smiles.

Onika is gazing out the window of the bus, and waves as she sees us driving up.

"Have a spectacular day," I say to my mom as I get out of the car. "I love you!"

"Love you most," she affirms and waits until the bus leaves before driving to work.

"Hey, Alyssa," greets Onika as I quickly walk towards our seats. "I didn't know you had to drive to the bus stop. Where do you live?"

"Oh, not too far from here," I say, and then change the subject to her very fashionable boots. They look very comfortable. They are purple, orange, and green and look very expensive. They have a fancy gold buckle on the side and white furry insides. She explains that the boots are a gift from her dad; he got them during one of his trips out of the country.

The bus chatter is extra loud this morning. Everyone is talking about something that happened on the news.

"Did you hear about that tornado," announces a snaggletooth kid. "It ripped apart over 356 houses! That's crazy insane!"

"No, it didn't! You are exaggerating!" yells a girl with blonde curly hair, calling him out on his outright lie. "The news said only 126 houses were damaged. It also destroyed an elementary school and hospital."

"Well, no matter how many houses it was" interrupts the boy with the missing tooth, "it's still crazy! And terrifying! Even one house is one too many!" All the kids nod in agreeance to that. No one would desire to reside in any of the affected houses.

"Alyssa, this is what I was telling you about yesterday. It appears the storm destroyed more homes than I knew. Our church and my dad's job are collecting items to send to the people affected. This situation is so sad."

During class, Ms. T. also discusses the tornado and remarks the PTO will donate supplies to the school that was damaged, and should any of us want to give items, we may drop them off this week. "The PTO will place a box at the front of the school to collect items."

While she is talking, I hear Marcus say under his breath, "I ain't giving nobody nothing; they didn't give me anything." He begins to write on his desk. He isn't a friendly kid.

Yellow Blouse

That evening, as Mom and I are having dinner, I tell her about the box for donations. Instead of reading right away, we decide to watch the news. Turning on the small TV, we hear the anchorwoman describing the loss of lives and property in Alabama, and they show footage of the places affected. I can see all the destruction. It looks identical to a warzone.

In disbelief, I ask, "Mom, are ALL those people homeless similar to us?"

"Yes, Alyssa, they are," she replies. "There are lots of reasons why people become homeless. Some are a result of natural disasters, such as what just happened in Alabama. Others, because of personal choices, as in addictions to drugs and alcohol. Still, others become homeless because of illnesses that cause families to get behind on their financial obligations, or mental health illnesses that make it difficult for the individual to make financial decisions without the aid of others."

"Similar to what occurred with us," I whisper.

My dad became sick and stayed home from work for a few days. When he didn't get any better, Mom scheduled an appointment for him to see his doctor. The news was not what we had hoped; his diagnosed was terminal. Initially, he was still receiving his paychecks from his job, because he had sick leave saved up. However, after being hospitalized for six months, my daddy died.

Mom handled most of the living expenses with the money they had in savings. When the savings ran out, she sold the items in our home. She started with the TV, our washer and dryer, then all the remaining furniture in the house. Finally, she sold Dad's car.

One day while getting off the school bus, the sheriff was standing at the house with papers in his hand explaining the bank now owned our home, and we only had a few hours to move out of the house. It was no longer ours. We gathered what few items we had remaining: clothes, pictures, some books. Packing it all into the two suitcases, Dad bought when he and Mom took their last vacation; we slid what remained of our lives into the trunk of Mom's car.

Mom is a hard worker, and when we lived with family members, she worked two jobs and overtime, but she could never make enough money to pay off the remaining hospital bills, plus put down a deposit and the first month's rent for a place.

That very moment, we were homeless. More homeless than when we were staying with friends and family. Homeless-homeless. Living in our car, homeless.

Mom predicts things will turn around soon. She emphasizes our need to be optimistic, and to do what we can with what we have, and be good stewards of our possessions. My mom has a very sunny disposition, as my dad would say. He adored how she would always find the silver lining in everything, even things that made her very sad.

Listening to the news, I ask if I can share something of mine with the children who have lost everything. Mom smiles and exclaims, "Of course." Together we go through my small drawer of belongings, and I select my favorite yellow blouse. It is the one thing that makes me smile when I wear it; it reminds me of my dad. Yellow was his favorite color.

When Mom sees me reaching for it, she places her hand over mine and asks, "Honey, are you sure you want to donate THIS one? It is your favorite shirt."

"Yes, I do. I want to give my best to those children who, similarly to us, have lost everything."

As soon as I say this, my mom lets go of my hand then tightly hugs me.

I immediately take my favorite blouse to the bathroom sink, to hand wash it then lay it out to dry across the tub. I don't want anything to happen to it before I can donate it. Mom turns off the TV, and we read a few pages before going to sleep.

That night, I say a prayer for the children in Alabama whose life echoes ours, homeless. I pray that whoever gets my favorite yellow blouse will wear it with pride and know someone was thinking of them.

Letting Go

That morning, I get on the bus from in front of the apartment building. It is the last stop, so everyone is already on board. When I get on, Onika is waving from our seats. She saved my place for me.

"Hey, girl! When I didn't see you, I thought you were sick or something," she elaborates while skootching nearer to the window. "Did you move? Why are you boarding the bus at this location?" she inquires as she studies the buildings.

"Thank you for saving my seat," I say, not answering her question. I don't know if she recognizes the apartment and knows that it is a shelter. "My mom had to leave early for work," I say, "so I told her I would get on the bus here; it is close to her job." I am not lying. My mom does work close by the shelter, just a few blocks away, and she did have to leave early for work.

Onika shows me all the supplies her folks bought to go in the donation box for the children. She has new crayons, pencils, fruit-scented markers, and loads of new books and folders. When she asks what I brought, I tell her that I brought something special for them and that I will put it in the box when we arrive at school. I dislike having to be so secretive, but I can't take the chance of letting anyone know my situation. Hopefully, one day, I will be honest and share everything with my new best friend. But not today. Not just yet, anyway.

Placing our things into our lockers, she asks if I want to eat breakfast. I tell her that I need to go to the bathroom first. That's not a lie. I do have to go, but I also want to drop off my blouse without anyone seeing.

I walk towards the bathroom then take an immediate turn to the left. I quickly grab the blouse from my bookbag in my locker then dash to the front hall. As I get ready to place my prized possession into the box, just holding it near the table causes my hands to tremble and tears well up in my eyes. I want to donate it, I do! But seeing it hovering over the box reminds me that once I let go of it, I will never see it or my daddy again.

I hold the blouse close to my face as I whisper, "Daddy, I know you gave this to me, but someone else needs it more than I do. You always taught me that if I am giving something away, make sure it is something I would want to have. So, today, I am giving away the best that I possess."

I prepare myself to drop it in the box, and you will never believe my misfortune! Marcus, of all people, sneaks up from behind and startles me. I haven't had much to say to him since I started coming to this school, because he is mean.

"I just knew you were up to something!" he shouts. "You just looked sneaky! Are you stealing from the box? Wait, you aren't stealing! GROSS! You're giving away your old, used clothes! That's disgusting!" he yells as he runs towards the lunchroom. "I can't believe you are giving away your old stuff! My mom bought new stuff for those kids. Tell your mom to buy new stuff to give away. It's a donation box, not a trash can!"

Oh no, now what am I going to do? If Marcus goes in the lunchroom blabbering to everyone what I donated, I will never hear the end of it. I almost consider taking the blouse back to my locker but know that a little girl in Alabama needs it more than I do. I decide that I can take whatever comes my way, even if it is coming directly from that bully Marcus!

Making my way back into the lunchroom, Onika walks towards the door. "Girl, what took you so long? You missed all the excitement. Marcus came in ranting that someone is throwing used items into the box. I wonder who he is talking about. Did you see someone out there?"

Before I can respond to her questions, the warning bell rings, and we head to class. "Saved by the bell," I silently whisper.

Classroom Visitor

When we make our way to class, Ms. T. is already standing at the board. "Alright everyone, come in and quietly take your seats. We have a special speaker today who will share information regarding ways the PTO will assist the children in Alabama."

Settling into our seats, someone stands and walks to the front of the class, "Hello, students, my name is Christine Bush; I volunteer with the PTO as well as run a non-profit organization called Valoha."

welcome Mrs. Bush with
Valoha

"Mrs. Bush," inquires Kyle as he is raising his hand, "what does Vahoola mean?"

"Thank you for asking, and it is Valoha. Think of the word aloha with a v – Valoha. In Hawaii, 'Aloha' means a lot of things, such as hello, goodbye, love, compassion, peace, mercy, and affection. The 'v' is for value. Valoha is a 501(c)(3) non-profit organization that assists the homeless community.

"Mrs. Bush!" yells Shane, Kyle's best friend. Neither one of them ever waits until they are called upon to ask their questions; they both always blurt out stuff. "If Valoha is in Hawaii, why are you here discussing what happened in Alabama?" He looks over at Kyle and snickers.

Marcus responds, "Good one," and they fist bump.

"Thank you for asking," responds Mrs. Bush, seeming oblivious to their buffoonery, "we are here because our sponsors have donated supplies to send to the children in Alabama, the same as we do for the children in Hawaii."

"Should we only give NEW stuff?" yells out Marcus as he gives me the side-eye.

"All donations are welcome: new and previously owned. Children who have lost everything will appreciate anything given," she reassures. "If possible, it would be great to include a letter to the recipient. There is nothing more special than receiving a handwritten message from someone your age saying they are thinking of you." She concludes her speech by detailing the supplies sponsored by her organization and sponsors. She thanks us for our generosity and passes out informational flyers that we may take home to our parents. Once she leaves, it is business as usual.

The day goes by quickly, and as we are leaving, Ms. T. reminds us of our writing assignment. On the way to the bus, Onika asks if I had a chance to begin working on my paper yet. She started hers but is having a hard time thinking of something to write about; nothing is coming to mind. Onika indicates she is going to inquire if Ms. T. will allow her to write about something else, perhaps a trip she has taken or a new toy she has received.

"What are you going to write about?" she probes, "I bet, similar to me, you are having trouble thinking of something, and you want me to ask if we both can have a different assignment? Since I am asking, I may as well get permission for both of us!"

"I have several things I've been contemplating," I say, but don't go into too many details.

"I'm sure you will do a great job, no matter what you write about," she emphasizes. "Already I can tell that you go the extra mile!"

"To Busseyville and beyond!" I shout as I quickly point up to the sky.

"What does that mean?' she inquires.

"Oh, nothing," I say as I put my hand back into my lap, "just something my family quotes."

The bus ride is quieter than the other days. I think people are just tired. It has been a long week.

Last One On, First One Off

Since I am the last one to get on the bus in the morning, I am the first one to get off in the afternoon.

"Alyssa, I will see you tomorrow. Please call if you want to get together to work on our papers," insists Onika as I stand to leave.

"OK, I sure will," I reply as I exit the bus.

I wait until the bus pulls further up the road before I cross to the apartments. I am so busy looking for oncoming cars; I don't realize Marcus is peering out the back window. He sees me entering the apartment building.

When I get inside, I immediately lock the door behind me. "Mommy, are you here?" I call out. Not hearing a response, I unpack my bookbag and begin my homework. I have a few questions remaining by the time she arrives. She looks extra tired today, so I volunteer to make dinner.

I look inside the fridge and find some bologna, a cheese slice, and a few pieces of bread. I make us sandwiches, and we pretend we are on a picnic at the zoo. We pull the tattered blanket off the bed and put it onto the floor. As we sit and eat, we talk about all the make-believe animals we pretend to see walking around in the grass. I cherish spending time with my mom; she is such an exceptional person.

Afterward, we put the blanket back onto the bed, then I shower. The picnic may be imaginary, but thank goodness the shower is real. While brushing my hair, I tell Mom about Mrs. Bush and the letters she asked us to write. I mention that I want to write one because I know what firsthand the effects of homelessness, and I understand their fears personally. Mom agrees it would be a beautiful thing to do and confirms that should I decide to write one; she will review it for me.

After taking a few minutes to think it through, I sit at the small desk and begin to write:

Dear Student,

My name is Alyssa, and I am so sorry you are having a tough time right now. I know things must be terrifying for you and your family, with not having a house or school. If anyone's hurt because of the storm, I hope they get better quickly. I know you will get a lot of letters from other students, but I want you to know that I understand what you are going through.

About a year ago, my dad died, and since then, my mom and I have been struggling. At first, we were able to stay in our home, and I could still go to the same school and play with my old friends. Then, because of the hospital bills, my mom was not able to keep up with the payments, and the sheriff made us leave our home. My dad had insurance, but it was not enough to pay all the bills.

Right now, we are living in a shelter for mothers and children. I am going to a great school and have met some incredibly kind kids. They don't know I am homeless. I am not sure how they will treat me if they find out. I hope your friends are compassionate to you even though you are not living in your home. And I pray you can move back into your own home very soon.

Each night I pray the same thing for my mom and me. I will add you to my meditations. I know you don't know me, but I am your friend. Take care, and if you can, write me back. My name is Alyssa Bussey. I attend Lee Ponder Middle School and am in Ms. Thompson's class.

Bye for now, Alyssa

I show my mom my letter. She acknowledges I did a splendid job writing it, and she is so proud I used my best penmanship.

Folding the letter neatly, I slide it into a yellow envelope I find in the desk and then place it in my folder. I brush my mom's hair; it's my way of letting her know how much I appreciate her. We talk a little more until it is time to go to sleep.

I remember to say my night time affirmations...

A Sign Over The Door

That night, I dream I am living in a new house. It is a house I have never seen. Over the front door is a sign that reads, "There is No Place Like My Own Home." Everything in the house is brand spanking new. Mom stands in the kitchen, smiling. I am so happy that I begin to sing and dance. I must have started singing in my sleep because I hear Mom calling my name.

"Alyssa, are you OK?" she asks. "You are talking in your sleep."

"Sorry Mom, I was dreaming of us living in a brand-new house; you were looking inside the cabinets, and they contained all of our favorite foods!"

"Oh, that is a beautiful dream, sweetie," she replies. "Be sure to eat some sour gummy bears for me."

I try to go back to sleep but am too excited. I must have eventually drifted off because I wake up when I hear Mom in the kitchen preparing coffee. I push back the covers and get up. Stumbling into the tiny bathroom, I brush my teeth and get dressed for school.

Mom and I go over her schedule, and then I hug her before leaving the apartment to walk towards the bus stop. Mom watches me from outside the door until the bus comes. She then grabs her purse and drives to work.

As I am making my way past kids to get to my seat, Marcus is looking at me strangely, as if he has a secret or is holding something over me. Maybe he needs a laxative. It is making me feel nervous. He's such a mean kid. I sincerely hope he is extremely constipated! I chuckle at the thought.

"Hey, Alyssa," he utters with a smirk. Everyone looks at me as he snickers as if he wants me to respond.

Well, I'm super proud of my name — it is my granny's name — so I stare him right in the eye and say, "Hey, Marcus, you need something from me?" I make sure I pause with every word as if I am clapping between each one of them.

"Naw," he quips as he grins again, then taps the shoulder of the boy with glasses sitting next to him. They whisper and giggle the entire way to the school.

Onika advises I not worry about them; they are all idiots; she is staring them squarely in the eyes as she utters the word "idiots." I don't care about them, but I do want to know what they think is so darn funny. Wiping my hand across my face, I ask Onika if I have food in my teeth or a booger or something on my nose.

"Not at all; they are just miserable brats!" she accuses.

When we finally get to class, I reach in my bookbag to get my letter to give to Ms. T.

"Wait? Oh, My Goodness! Where is it?" I whisper. Frantically searching the bottom of my bag, I can't believe what I am seeing, or should I say, NOT seeing! It must be in here! Desperately, I look all over the floor near my seat and dig further into the bottom of my bag. I dump everything out onto my desk! It's not there! I feel tears starting to sting my eyes. I wrote my entire life story in that letter! It is not something I want floating around the school.

I raise my hand, and even before Ms. T. sees it, I blurt out, "Ms. T., may I please go look in the cafeteria for the letter that I wrote for the students in Alabama? It is not in my bag."

She looks at me a bit puzzled but ultimately answers yes. Jumping out of my seat as if my butt is on fire, I haul tail out the door! Everyone gawks at me, but I don't care. I must find that letter.

Just You Wait

Resembling a bloodhound, I retrace my steps back to the lunchroom, then to my locker. I even peer out the front door, searching to see if perhaps I dropped it on the ground as I was walking in from the bus.

I. Can't. Find. It. Anywhere!

I don't know what I am going to do.

I feel my stomach starting to churn.

It hurts so badly I am doubled over in pain.

Rather than head back to class, I go straight to the nurse's office.

Glancing up from her computer screen, Ms. Oglevie asks if everything is OK. I can't say anything. I start crying. Immediately, she comes over and sits down beside me. She pats my back, waiting patiently for the faucet of tears to subside. Finally, I catch my breath. Suspecting that I am done crying and not just taking a break, Ms. Oglevie asks if I can explain what happened. I gather my voice and share that I lost something vitally important to me, something that contains personal information.

"It has confidential stuff that I don't want others to discover." Then the waterfall returns. This time, it produces a flood.

I must have been crying so much she felt she needed to call in the guidance counselor for reinforcement. Mrs. Beck also allows me to get all my tears out, then asks if there is anything at all she may do to assist me.

I open my mouth to speak, but nothing comes out. Mimicking a bobblehead doll, I shake my head no. Mrs. Beck gives me a tissue to wipe my face and blow my nose, then gives me a letter to take home to my mom, saying she came in to see me. Ms. Oglevie gives me a pass back to class and advises, "Alyssa, whatever it is that you've lost, it will turn up. Please, let me know if there is anything Mrs. Beck or I can do for you."

Angrily, I make my way through halls that once felt safe and comfortable, but now seem empty and cold! I know they hold the secret to where the letter is and are playing a cruel, sick game with me. Secret? Wait for just one minute!

Maybe!

No!

He couldn't have!

I suddenly recall the way Marcus was eyeing me when I got on the bus. I wonder if he saw me drop the letter and distracted me until one of his goonies could pick it up.

"Oh, you wait until I get back to class. You want to be a bully, do you? Then, buddy, I'm the matador! You ain't seen nothing yet."

Easy Isn't Best and Best Isn't Easy

With arms flailing in front of me as if I am passing a baton in a relay race, I practically run to class and head full speed towards his desk. It's confrontation time! Marcus sees me coming, throws both his hands up in front of his face and yells, "Whoa, what did I do?"

Seething, I open my mouth to attack him verbally, and that's when I see it! Only Marcus doesn't have it. Out the corner of my eye, I see Maya, our bus driver looking directly at me. In her hand, I see a bright yellow envelope, identical to the one I put my letter in. Can it be?

"Alyssa, could you please come to my desk?" insists Ms. T.

I was ogling so intently at the yellow envelope in Maya's hand that I didn't hear Ms. T. the first time. She repeats herself. "Alyssa, did you hear me? Please come to my desk." Now everyone is watching me!

With my hands behind my back and my shoulders slouched forward, I make my way slowly to her desk. "Ms. T., I can explain… I couldn't find an item that is significant to me… and I got sick… so I went to the nurse's office…here is the pass she gave me, allowing me to return to class," I say it all so quickly, it sounds as if it's one gigantic mangled sentence.

"Thank you for the pass, Alyssa," she calmly responds. "Maya found this on the bus and believes it may belong to you."

Suspended in mid-air between her two-inch-long, blinged-out fingernails, is my bright yellow envelope. What? How's this possible? Marcus is innocent! He didn't have it after all. I drop my head in shame as I feel the heat rising to my cheeks. I jumped to conclusions, didn't I? I blamed Marcus. In my fear, I allowed myself to have negative thoughts towards him, and he was not at fault. Pushing all that aside, I reach out my shaking hand for the letter, I whisper, "Thank you so much, Maya, I was looking for this. I thought I had lost it."

"Alyssa, you dropped it as you were exiting this morning," reveals Maya, "I couldn't bring it in right away because I had to move the bus from the front of the school. Once I parked, I brought it right in."

This letter has already caused more trouble than it is worth; I consider tearing it into a million tiny pieces. I am no longer sure I want someone knowing all my business. If I felt this horrible thinking it was lost, how will I react knowing someone read it?

Folding it in my hands, I make my way back to my desk. Then suddenly, I hear my dad's voice in my head, "Ali, easy things aren't always the best things, and the best things aren't always easy."

Turning back towards them, I say, "Thank you, Maya, for bringing my letter to me." Then I return and place the envelope on Ms. T.'s desk, "This is my letter for a student in Alabama. Could you send it to them with the donated items?"

Afterward, I lift my chin, hold out my chest, and with my head high, I walk back to my seat.

I was in the nurse's office so long I didn't realize half the day has passed. The bell rings for us to go to lunch. While eating meatloaf and mashed potatoes, Onika declares, "Girl, the way you stormed into the class heading straight for Marcus, I thought for sure you were going to rip his head off! What in the world happened?"

"I thought he took something that belonged to me," I say while eating my salad, "I really should have waited until I had more information before rushing to judgment," I tell her how losing it made me feel sad inside. "It was the letter I wrote to a student in Alabama. I took my time writing it out and am very proud of it. Now that I located it, I feel much better."

"Oh wow, you already wrote your letter?" she asks. "I can't even think of anything to write, and you finished your letter? You are so good with getting your assignments completed. I need to learn how to finish my projects as you do! I am glad you are my friend. You are going to help me to get my act together."

When we return to class, Mrs. Beck and Mrs. Bush are in the class talking to Ms. T. They both look up and then leave just as we walk in.

"Everyone, please go to the blackboard wall and select a smiley-face rock from the basket then go to the carpet area."

One by one, we select a rock, then make our way to the center of the room and sit down on the floor. I look in my hand and see the word resilient written on it. On the opposite side is a face with a winky eye. The word is perfect for me. As we sit, Ms. T. asks us to share the word we have selected and how it relates to our day.

Raising her hand, Cierra asks if she may go first.

"Absolutely," responds Ms. T.

"My word is unlimited, and I feel this relates to my potential. I have unlimited potential."

"Very good," affirms Ms. T., "anyone else?"

"I would appreciate going next," requests Daymeon. "My word is intentional, and I believe this means in everything I do, I have to be deliberate in my efforts."

"Excellent responses," she indicates, then goes around the room allowing the students to comment on the rock they've selected briefly. After each person shares, we return the stones to the basket and begin our math assignments.

The end of day bell rings before I know it and we all pile out the door and unto the bus.

To Busseyville And Beyond

I am not in a very talkative mood but am glad to listen to Onika as she chatters the entire way home. I am so happy I met her.

When I arrive home, I mean to the shelter, I don't see my mom waiting, so I use my key to go in. I find a note on the small table near the door,

> "Ali, I will be a little late today. I left food in the fridge for you. Please be sure to double-check the locks before you begin your homework, and I will see you later.
>
> Love you most, Mom."

Checking and rechecking the locks on the door, I make a snack, then start my homework. As I am writing, I remember the emotions I had when I thought I'd lost the letter. I wonder if I want to write about my real life, or similar to Onika, write about something else. As I close my eyes, contemplating, I hear my dad's voice in my head, "Ali, remember, we are Busseys. We don't take the easy way out. We always go over, above, and beyond! To Busseyville and beyond!"

"To Busseyville and beyond!" I say out loud. Just as I do, my mom walks in the door. She looks crazy tired. I hate that she must work so hard. I wish there were something I could do to make things better for her.

"Hey, Mommy."

The sound of her keys hitting the counter reminds me of how fortunate we are to no longer have to sleep in our car, if only temporarily so.

"Hey, Sunshine. Guess what happened today?" Mom asks as she sits to unlace her sneakers. I glance at them and realize her shoes are older than my bookbag.

"What happened?" I ask, desperate to hear some good news.

"One of my regulars came to the restaurant discussing online classes that certify medical coders. She felt I would be great at it and said coders work from home. It pays enough that we will be able to afford a new place to live."

Jumping up to hug her, I say, "That is wonderful news! And of course, I will contribute towards the completion of your assignments! I am good at homework."

"Indeed, you are," she agrees. We talk about the course and how it will significantly improve things for us.

Listening to the excitement in my mom's voice causes me to forget all about losing the letter and my trip to the nurse's office. It is only after taking a shower that I recall the events. During our reading time, I tell her all about it. She indicates how sorry she is that I lost the letter and had a hard time finding it. She hugs me and reminds me of all that is wonderful about me. I cherish my mom!

The next morning, while getting on the bus, I feel as if things are changing for the better, things are finally looking up.

"Hey, Alyssa," retorts Marcus.

Maybe things aren't as rosy as I believe.

"What do you want, Marcus?" I ask, trying to be mindful of my tone because of falsely accusing him yesterday, even if he doesn't know it.

"Tell us about your house. Where do you live?" he smirks as he asks this question.

Everyone looks at me as if I grew a horn in the center of my head.

"She doesn't have to tell you anything. Who died and made you the housing commissioner?" chides Onika. "Don't listen to him; he's a miserable person. He is just mad at life and doesn't know how to deal with his own. Isn't that right, Marcus?" When she voices this, he looks down at his feet. Now everyone is looking at him as if he grew the horn. I don't know what Onika is referring to, but apparently, he knows, and for once, he is quiet.

When we get to class, there are tripods towards the front of the room. They have information about resources for housing, etc. Seeing posters depicting homelessness causes me to squirm just a bit. I hope all the additional attention on the subject is not due to my situation or my letter. I don't think Maya and Ms. T. read my letter; now I am not so sure. Uncertain, I take my seat with the rest of my class while taking deep breaths to calm my nerves.

Livable For Everyone

"Good morning, everyone. I hope you all had a great night's sleep and are ready to receive wisdom and knowledge this wonderful new day. Today, we are fortunate to have Mr. Robert Doss, Jr., here to speak to us. He is touring our district to discuss National Homelessness, Hunger, and Poverty Awareness. Considering the recent events that took place in Alabama, Principal Bell invited him to come to spend a few minutes with each class to answer any questions we may have. Please give Mr. Doss your undivided attention as you may utilize what you learn to complete your writing assignment. It may also encourage you to understand our Social Studies lessons for this quarter."

Mr. Doss is tall, with a shiny bald head and a bright smile. He has a pleasant voice, and has a lot of knowledge about resources, primarily through an organization called Homes for the Homeless.

"Mr. Doss," asks Melissa, "what does Homes for the Homeless do?"

"The mission of Homes for the Homeless is to provide housing to those who do not have shelter."

"What sort of housing? Are they similar to mobile homes or tiny houses?" she asks.

"The houses are simple homes that are sometimes new or previously built. They are not luxury homes, but are decent and affordable."

"Since you provide new homes, who builds them?" asks Onika.

"That is a wonderful question. We have volunteers who work with our organization as well as volunteers within the community where we are building. Also, the family receiving the home assists in building it as well."

"That resembles an awful lot of work. Why do the people who get the homes have to participate in the process? Aren't there volunteers for situations such as this?" asks Daymeon.

"It is work; however, many inform us, it is fun as well. We have found that people who assist in the building of their homes take pride in ownership and become wonderful homeowners," declares Mr. Doss.

"Other than to build houses, are there things we may do as children?" asks Kimble.

"I am so glad you asked. Yes, there are things you may do to assist your neighbors. You may have a Community Closet-Cleaning Day; this is when you clean out your closet of usable items and then donate them to shelters or set up the items in a central area with tags that say, "free."

"That is a wonderful idea!" expresses Ms. T., "what other suggestions do you recommend?"

"You may fill shoeboxes with toiletries items such as toothbrush, toothpaste, soap, small bottles of shampoo, crackers, and snacks, then with an adult, pass them out or take them to local shelters."

"I enjoy playing my guitar," admits Cierra, "could I give lessons to a child? Music always makes me smile."

"Indeed, we have youth who give music lessons, sports lessons and teach arts and crafts. There are shelters in the area that allow children to come to spend an afternoon with other kids their age."

All the students begin to raise their hands, telling Mr. Doss all their talents and abilities.

"Class, I am glad you are excited; however, Mr. Doss cannot answer questions he cannot understand. Kindly use your classroom manners."

"Yes, Ms. T.," we respond.

Darryl raises his hand, "Mr. Doss, you said your organization provides homes for individuals who are without shelter, what is the process for getting a new home?"

"We believe in providing homes that are livable for everyone…"

"Livable for everyone?" I ask, without even realizing the words are coming out of my mouth.

"Yes, livable for everyone. We have offices all over the U.S."

"Who just gives away brand new homes?" blurts out Marcus. That kid needs to learn classroom manners. Wait. What am I saying? I just shouted out my question, too. I guess, in this case, we both need etiquette lessons.

"That is a great question," suggests Mr. Doss. "We don't just give the homes away. Homes for the Homeless is a hand-up program, not a hand-out. Who knows what the difference is?"

"It means the organization is designed to aid people to become more self-sufficient," responds Daymeon, "and not just give them things, such as a house. So, does that mean they have to work for it?"

"My dad states completion of my chores are my way of earning things that I want," declares Onika. "For instance, you see my boots and clothes? Well, I had to do extra chores around the house for these. Well, not these boots, my dad brought these from his business trip."

"That is a great example," expounds Mr. Doss, "the family puts in 350 hours."

"Does the family have to pay the mortgage for the new home?" queries Ms. T.

"Yes, they do! Approved families do not pay interest, but they do have a monthly payment. Paying allows them to own their home eventually, and when people earn things, we have found they take better care of them."

"Students, please thank Mr. Doss for coming to share with us."

"Thank you, Mr. Doss," we say in unison as he packs his items to go and speak with the other classrooms. He leaves flyers on the table that we may take home to our parents.

When the lunch bell rings, Ms. T. asks if I may stay behind to go over something with her.

Onika looks at me as if I did something incorrectly. "Is everything OK?"

I shrug my shoulders. "I don't know why they wouldn't be. Perhaps Ms. T. simply wants to discuss my letter since I turned it in yesterday." But inwardly I hope it is NOT about my letter.

"Alyssa," she declares after all the students are out of the room, "First

I want to say it was coincidental that Mr. Doss stopped by our class today. However, I read your letter, and I have a few questions for you."

I look at her, not sure what she is about to ask me. "OK, Ms. T."

"First, you wrote a beautiful letter; your penmanship and attention to detail are amazing. I am so proud of the obvious time and effort you put into your letter. I am sure whoever acquires it will be happy to read it. But I wanted to ask if the information you mentioned is truthful or if some of the information is fictional. You know, make-believe, intended to encourage the reader to feel better about their circumstances."

I am not sure how to answer her question. Am I in trouble for writing my personal information? Were we not supposed to put our real names in the letter? Our school? Our teacher's name. I decide to answer the best way I know how, with the truth.

And Nothing But The Truth

"Ms. T., everything in the letter is real. It is all factual. Did I say something I was not supposed to say?"

"Not at all, I just wanted to verify the information before mailing it," she admits, "you may go get your lunch. If you need extra time eating, don't rush, just come to class when finished. Here is a hall pass should you need it."

I leave to join Onika in the cafeteria. She is waiting for me with my lunch on the table when I walk in. She is such a good friend.

"I got your lunch for you. I told Mrs. Green, you had to stay after, and she wanted to be sure you ate. What did Ms. T. want? Did you do something wrong? What am I saying? Of course, you didn't do anything wrong! Maybe you did something right, as in exceptionally correct, and she wanted to give you extra credit. Listen to me, blabbering. I'm sorry, you can't even answer since I'm talking so much."

"You make me laugh, Onika! I didn't do anything wrong. Ms. T. had questions about the letter I wrote and wanted to clarify before it was mailed off."

"Oh, is that all! Well, I am glad to hear that it isn't anything serious."

We eat our lunch and head back to class.

When I get home, I take my items out of my bookbag and see a letter with Ms. T.'s handwriting addressed to my mom. I place it in plain sight on the counter for my mom to see when she arrives home from work.

Later, after dropping her purse on the chair, she opens the letter, and we sit at the small table reading it.

Ms. Bussey,

I want first to say it is an absolute joy having Alyssa in my class. She is very attentive and takes exceptional care in her work. Recently, she wrote an inspiring message to a student in Alabama. It is because of this letter that I want to invite Alyssa and you to come in for a meeting.

I know with your work schedule it may be a bit challenging to come in during the day, so I am available to meet after school. My phone number is listed below, and I look forward to meeting with you.

Sincerely,

Ms. Odette Thompson

555-422-9611

We look up at each other and then back at the letter. Mom isn't quite sure what to make of it but stipulates she will come to my classroom tomorrow after school, to wait for her there, and not to get on the bus.

After supper, we shower and then read for a few minutes and go to sleep. My sleep is fretful; I guess I am a bit anxious about the meeting after school. I don't know what to make of it.

The next morning, there is an envelope on the kitchen floor. Someone must have slipped it under the door last night.

"Not another letter! What is it with people sending me notes?" Mom sighs, as she slowly treads over to get it.

This time, reading it causes her to smile, and not just smile, but beam. "It is from the manager of the shelter. It contains the most excellent news! The committee revealed we may reside here for an extra 90 days past our initial stay."

"Does this mean we will be here for six whole months?" I squeal while doing my happy dance.

"I haven't seen you make those moves in a long time," she laughs, as she too dances around the tiny space. "This will allow us to save enough money to get our apartment finally! I will also be able to take the classes for medical coding, and you can keep riding the same bus to school. It seems as if things are finally looking up for us. To Busseyville and beyond!"

After we finish our poorly choreographed happy dance, she reiterates, "Be sure to not get on the bus after school today; I will meet you there."

As I walk out the door, I say, "Love you, Mom. Have a wonderful day."

"I love you most. I will meet you at your school later."

Looking both ways, I cross the street just as the bus is approaching.

Once onboard, I hear Onika calling out to me, "Hey, Alyssa." As I get closer, she moves over near the window so I may sit down, "How are you today?"

"Doing great, how about you?" But, before she may respond, I say, "Oh, wow! I adore your scarf, is that new?" I reach out to touch it, and it feels so luxurious and delicate. Similar to what I imagine, a spider's web would resemble if you could make a scarf out of it. No, not a spider's web, more similar to dove's feathers. Yeah, dainty along those lines.

"Yes, it is a hand-painted silk shawl from Thailand. My dad brought it back from his business trip. Isn't it beautiful?"

"It is fantabulous! I say.

We chat while walking into the building about the travels her dad does for his job. It sounds exciting, I can't fathom getting paid real money to visit exotic locations such as Italy, Spain, Turkey. I listen intently to all her stories. When her father travels during the summer months, she and her mom accompany him. She explains she has photo albums jam-packed with pictures of her during her visits. Hearing them make me smile outwardly, but inwardly, I am sad too. Listening to her talk about her father causes me to miss mine. For now, though, I am celebrating with my best friend.

After School Meeting

After school, as everyone leaves for the bus, Onika asks if I am coming too.

"I have a meeting with Ms. T. and my mom," I tell her as she grabs her things to go.

"OK. See you tomorrow."

As I sit at my desk, waiting for my mom to arrive, Ms. T. is at hers, working on papers.

"Ms. T., am I in trouble?"

"No, not at all," she reassures, then smiles. "You are a model student. I want to meet with your mom and you to go over some things. Mr. Doss will also join us. You remember him, right?"

"He is the man who spoke about Homes for the Homeless?"

"Yes," she confirms.

While still speaking, my mom walks in.

"Hey Mom," I say, greeting her with a hug.

As Ms. T. and Mom shake hands, I notice how tired my mom looks. I didn't realize it early; she

appears a bit worried.

We sit down at the round table near Ms. T.'s desk. As we do, Mr. Doss walks in. Shaking our hands, he introduces himself to Mom. "Hello, my name is Mr. Doss, and I work with Homes for the Homeless. I am here to talk to you about our organization and to discuss ways we may be able to provide shelter for you and Alyssa. Is it OK if I have a seat?"

"Please," invites my mom. "Thank you for asking me to come and for sharing your information with me. I assume you read the letter Alyssa wrote. I am so proud of her. She wrote that from her heart; those are her very own words."

"Alyssa is an amazing writer, indeed," echoes Ms. T.

"Since you have read the letter, you are already mindful of our current living situation." Mr. Doss and Ms. T. both nod their heads. I reach over and hold Mom's hand when I hear her voice beginning to shake. "My husband, Edwin, was a wonderful man. He worked very hard every day of his life. He didn't make a lot of money, but we lived a beautiful, adventurous life. Our home had laughter, affection, and peace. When he first got sick, we didn't know what was going on with him. After a six-month hospital stay, sadly, he died." Mom pauses here to catch her breath, then continues, "His insurance didn't cover the hospital stay, the bills became too much for me to handle on my own, and we eventually became homeless."

My mom takes out a tissue from her purse and wipes her eyes.

Families Like Ours

"Mrs. Bussey, I am so sorry you lost your husband, and Alyssa, your dad. Our organization supports families similar to yours. We build homes for those in need. Upon being notified of Alyssa's letter, I discussed it with our staff, and they have unanimously agreed they can accommodate your housing needs. Are you in a safe place now? I know the letter indicates you are in a temporary shelter. How much longer will you be allowed to remain there?"

"We received a letter this morning saying we can stay for a total of six months. I also have been accepted into a training program that will facilitate in me get a better job in a few months, so things are starting to look up for us finally."

"Well, if you will allow us to, I would welcome the opportunity to build you and your daughter a new home. There are requirements on your part. You will have to attend classes designed to encourage you to be a responsible homeowner," he emphasizes.

"And, Mom, you and I will receive assistance in building it, we will put in sweet equality," I say.

"Sweat equity," he corrects me. "Yes, you and Alyssa will participate in building your new home. It is 350 hours of work, and you will also have a payment, but your mortgage is interest-free, and the payments are affordable."

"Will it be in this school district? Alyssa adores this school and you, Ms. T. I would hate to have to put her in a new school," Mom chokes out between tears.

Hearing my mom say how much I adore the school causes Ms. T. to reach across the table and pat my mom's hand. Even she has tears in her eyes.

"Absolutely," assures Mr. Doss. "We have lots of property in this district, and not too far from her bus stop. She will be able to ride the same bus if she would wish."

They talk a little bit more, then Mr. Doss stands and gives my mom his contact information. They set up a time to meet later. After he leaves, Ms. T. boasts about my progress and shares how proud she is to have me in her class.

On the way back to the shelter, we stop for ice cream sundaes. My mom has so much on her mind. At first, she sits quietly, deep in thought. Then finally she acknowledges, "Alyssa, had you not been so honest with your letter and wrote what you did, we would not have gotten this opportunity. I am so very proud of you."

I hug my mom, as we cry happy tears and enjoy our dessert.

Chin Up, Chest Out, Head High

When I arrive in class the next day, I ask Ms. T. if I may share my letter as my writing assignment with the students. Surprised, she indicates I do not have to do this if I don't want to. I reassure her it is something I need to do.

I hear my dad's voice in my mind encouraging me to be brave and aim for Busseyville! I clear my throat, lift my chin, hold my chest out, and hold my head high, then using my most courageous voice, begin speaking. "Ms. T. gave us a writing assignment that is due next week. In it, we were told to describe a difficult situation we have had and the steps we took to bring resolution.

You all know my name, but what you may not know is that my dad became very sick and died." I pause to catch my breath. "My mom tried

very hard to keep up with all the bills, but just couldn't. After a few months, we lost our house and became homeless. We lived with friends and family when we could. We even lived in our car." I look at Onika, who is just gawking into space; frozen in her chair. "We were fortunate to get space in a shelter for women and children, which is why I had to change bus stops, but it is only temporary. My mom works very hard, sometimes overtime, but she doesn't make enough money for us to get our place. The shelter gave us an extension so that we could stay there a bit longer, but it is not permanent." I pause again and see Onika looking confused, but I must continue. I have come too far to stop now. "Yesterday, Mr. Doss from Homes for the Homeless met with us to share that his organization will be building us a new house. He affirms it will be close to the bus stop, so I won't have to change schools or buses; I will still be able to come here and ride the bus with my friends."

I smile at Onika, who is now trying to blink back tears as she silently whispers, "Hey girl, HEY!"

"Mr. Doss found out about my story when I wrote this letter to a student in Alabama sharing that I understand being homeless. I even donated my favorite yellow blouse — the one my dad bought me — by placing it in the collection box." As I say this, I see a wide-eyed Marcus sheepishly hang his head.

Onika looks over at him. She knows now that I am the one, he was ranting about, and she gives him a furious look. He looks away quickly. Then as if he has received a bolt of revelation, raises his hand.

"Ms. T, didn't Mr. Doss say when they build homes, the community comes out to assist in expediting the process?"

"He did say that," confirms Ms. T.

"Well, since we collected items for the students in Alabama, can't we do the same for Alyssa and her mom for their new home? Is it possible that we can all pitch in and contribute to their sweat equity?"

Ms. T. smiles at him. Onika jumps clean out of her seat and runs full speed over to his desk. He throws his hands up and yells, "Whoa, what did I do?" just as she gives him a huge bear hug!

Hands go up, and everyone explains they too want to contribute towards building our house, that they have things they want to give. Ms. T. allows time for some Q and A but advises we must continue with our lessons.

As soon as my bottom hits my chair, Onika takes off her new scarf. "I want to give this to you. It isn't yellow, but I hope you'll accept it. I am so sorry about your dad. I regret that I didn't know what was going on with you. Now I know why you wouldn't accept my invitation to come over or didn't want me at your place to do our homework. I hope now we can change that."

"That sounds awesome; I will ask my mom," I say, and then we begin our work.

Community Affair

Time passes quickly; before we know it, it's time to begin building our new house. It is in the same neighborhood as Onika's home; I will be able to ride my bike over. Ms. Oglevie gave it to me. She heard about the letter and remembered the day I came to her office crying. The bike previously belonged to her niece, Jessica, who only used it when she came to visit; she is now too old for it. It is a perfect fit for me.

Everyone we know arrives to facilitate in building our house. It is heartwarming to see the entire community come together! Even my mom's boss and some of the ladies she works with arrive and assist. With lots of support from so many people, we will complete our Sweat Equity quickly. People we don't even know come and lend a hand of assistance. Once the house is complete and we finally get the keys to our new home, the very first thing Mom and I are going to do is hang the sign over our door that she received as a pre-housewarming gift. It reads, "There Is No Place Like Our Own Home."

Epilogue

It's been many years since the day we moved into our home. During the time of construction, Mom completed her classes and became a certified medical coder; she later became a Register Nurse. Before moving in, Mom received a job offer to be a coder that allowed her to work from home; she joined our PTO and is still a room mom to this day. She and Ms. T. are best friends. And, you will never believe what I found one day while walking around our backyard with Mom. I spotted a painted smiley face rock! Immediately, I picked it up and read, "Welcome Home," with a tiny red heart.

I am now grown and living in my own home — I kept the smiley face rock and proudly display it on my deck. Marcus turned out to not be such a brat after all. We began dating in high school and are now married and parents of twins, Onika and Owen. Onika and I are still best friends and live only minutes away from each other. We get together often; even our children are best friends. I will always remember the day I received a writing assignment that opened the door for all that followed. My mom's favorite saying is, "As long as we have breath, we have everything we will ever need." I teach this saying to my children. Mom and I are beyond blessed because, we do, indeed, have everything we will ever need.

The End.

Made in the USA
Columbia, SC
02 December 2022

72320034R00052